VOYAGERS!

Joe Claro

SCHOLASTIC BOOK SERVICES
New York Toronto London Auckland Sydney Tokyo

ISBN 0-590-32740-2

Copyright © 1982 by MCA Publishing, a Division of MCA Communications, Inc. All rights reserved. Published by Scholastic Book Services, a division of Scholastic Inc., by arrangement with MCA Publishing, a Division of MCA Communications, Inc.

12 11 10 9 8 7 6 5 4 3 2 1   10   2 3 4 5 6/8

Printed in the U.S.A.   06

VOYAGERS!

Chapter 1 _____

The screams of frightened peasants filled the air. They blended with the clank of sword against sword and the occasional whoop of delight from a pirate setting fire to a building.

All these sounds were drowned out every few seconds by a cannon blast from the pirate ship standing in the harbor. The pirates were here to loot the island of its gold. In the process, they might also free the island from British rule.

Six pirates raced out of a two-story building into the marketplace. In the lead was their cabin boy, Jeff, who carried a bag of gold coins taken from a strongbox in the building.

Four British soldiers raced out after the pirates, relieved to be out of the burning building. The soldiers brandished their swords over their heads and screamed curses at the pirates.

"Captain!" Jeff shouted.

Jeff and the men reached the center of the marketplace and stopped. Six more soldiers were coming at them from the front.

Thinking fast, Jeff got behind a vegetable cart and tipped it into the square. That slowed the oncoming soldiers long enough to allow the pirates to dash into another building.

Seconds later, they could be seen backing out onto the veranda of the second story of the building. Each pirate was engaged in a sword fight with a British soldier. Jeff had two to contend with.

The British army in the seventeenth century had some of the best swordsmen in the world. An ordinary swordsman couldn't last long against one such soldier. Fending off two together called for the skills of a world-class expert.

Jeff not only kept the two soldiers busy. He also scanned the general chaos below. Then he found what he was looking for.

There stood the pirate captain and a woman, cowering against the outside wall of a burning building. The flames licked around them while the captain fought off three British soldiers.

Jeff lunged with his sword, causing both the soldiers to back off. He used the few seconds left to give his full attention to the impending disaster below.

The captain and the woman both shot a glance in his direction. She looked up at Jeff gratefully. The captain, his attention back on the three swords threatening to finish him off, responded with a fierce yell.

"Give us a hand, son!" the captain pleaded. "Hurry!"

Jeff ducked to the side, avoiding a sword headed straight for his heart. Still holding his own sword, he leaped up and grasped an awning bar with both hands.

He swung his body back, lifted his feet in the air, and then shot forward in the direction of the chins of the two soldiers.

Both soldiers fell back, off the veranda and onto a tomato cart below. Jeff dropped to the veranda and grabbed a clothesline that would carry him down to the captain.

"Hurry, son!" the captain yelled. "I can't hold them off much longer!"

Holding the clothesline, Jeff left the veranda and sailed into space. A British soldier stepped into the spot Jeff had just left. Grinning, the soldier lifted his sword and hacked at the clothesline.

Jeff looked back in horror as the rope came free. Falling to the ground, he reached out his hands toward the captain.

"Father!" Jeff screamed.

The bedroom was dark and silent. "Father," Jeff said softly. Then he opened his eyes. He turned his body a little to the left, and his book fell to the floor.

Pirates in History, it was called. Jeff had been reading it when he fell asleep.

The thump of the book on the floor startled

him out of the dream. It also woke his dog, Ralph, who had been sleeping at the foot of the bed.

Ralph stirred and lifted his head. Jeff sighed, climbed off the bed, and opened the blinds. The sunlight hurt his eyes, so he closed the blinds and switched on a small light.

He picked up his book and carried it to his wall-length bookcase. He slipped the book into its empty space on a shelf that was jammed with other history books.

Then he stared at the photograph on the top shelf. It showed the cabin boy, the captain, and the woman. But they were wearing twentieth-century clothes. The burning building and the pirate ship were replaced by a suburban house and a lawn.

Jeff sighed again and threw himself back onto the bed. He could hear his Aunt Elizabeth in the living room talking with her boyfriend Tom.

Jeff had been living with her for eight months, since his parents had died in an auto accident. She wasn't crazy about the arrangement. A single woman doesn't like to get stuck with somebody else's eleven-year-old kid.

Jeff wasn't crazy about it either. But Aunt Elizabeth was his only relative.

He'd been given the choice of staying with her or trying his luck with foster parents. It wasn't much of a choice—for either of them. But they'd both agreed to try it out.

Now she was out there, probably arguing with Tom about taking on the responsibility of an orphan. He thought about opening the door and listening. But he'd heard it all before. He didn't feel like hearing it again.

He wiped a tear away with his sleeve and closed his eyes. Then he heard a rattling sound at the window. Ralph, the world's worst watchdog, jumped up on the bed for protection.

There was the rattling noise again. Jeff got up, walked to the window, and raised the blinds. Just as he did, a huge hand smashed through the window, holding a thick black book.

Jeff tried to shout, but no sound came out. A booted foot kicked out the rest of the glass. Jeff looked away to protect his face from the flying glass.

When he turned back, he saw a six-foot man wearing a getup that might have been put together by a costume designer gone mad.

Jeff had already seen the pirate boots, and he recognized them as seventeenth-century Spanish. Tucked into the boots was a pair of dueling pants, probably from eighteenth-century France.

Running from the waist up and over the shoulders was a gun belt. Jeff guessed that it was once worn by one of Pancho Villa's men in Mexico. The man's chest was bare, and the crisscross gun belt covered most of a saber scar.

Over the gun belt, he wore a leather vest that Jeff couldn't identify at all. It was probably from ancient England. All this was partly covered by a coat like the one Napoleon wore, though it was moth-eaten and dirty.

All together, he looked like a combination of every adventure movie hero Jeff had ever seen.

Except for his face. Two things about the man's face struck Jeff immediately. The first was that he might bear an eerie resemblance to the man in the photo on Jeff's bookcase.

The second was that it was the most frightened face Jeff had seen in a long time. The face was pale white, and the eyes bulged in fear, as the man looked out the broken window into the thirty-story drop to the ground.

"Smoking bat's breath!" he said in a stage whisper. "That fall could have killed me!"

He turned to face Jeff, who stood gaping and holding Ralph by the collar. Ralph had never faced any real danger before, and Jeff wasn't sure how the dog would react to all this.

"When did they start building them this high?" the man boomed at Jeff.

Ralph began to growl, and Jeff tightened his grip on the collar. The man looked around the room.

"Wait a minute!" he said. "This isn't 1492. Where's Columbus? Where am I?"

He began to stride into the room. At his

first step, Ralph broke free and leaped at the intruder.

"Ralph!" Jeff called. "Down!"

But Ralph's sense of danger to his master was stronger than his sense of obedience. He bared his teeth and did all he could to bring the man to the floor.

"Hey!" the man yelled. "Get him off!"

Jeff rushed over and yanked at Ralph's collar. The dog had gripped the man's black book in his teeth, and he was too heavy for Jeff to pull.

"He has my book!" the man screamed, trying to free himself from Ralph and Jeff.

"Ralph!" Jeff said. "Let go!"

As they struggled, the man threw out an arm that hit Jeff instead of Ralph. The force sent Jeff backing toward the window. He lost his balance and began to teeter backward.

The man had his book now. He turned and saw what was happening to Jeff. Forgetting everything else, he dropped the book and leaped to save Jeff.

Jeff was already too far out the window. That, and the man's forward motion sent them both plummeting toward the street.

As their screams quickly faded, Ralph went to the window, put his paws on the sill, and looked down.

There was nothing there. The space between the window and the street was empty. Thirty stories below, the traffic moved as it had been doing.

Jeff and the strange visitor had disappeared. Ralph whimpered. Then he turned back into the apartment and sniffed at the book the man had left behind.

Chapter 2 _____

Jeff had his eyes closed tight. He had stopped screaming, but he was still falling. Somehow, though, it didn't really feel like falling—not like the feeling he'd had in his pirate dream.

It was more like sailing—or floating. He opened his eyes slowly. He might be spinning as he fell, but he couldn't be sure. There was nothing he could focus his eyes on to see how he was moving.

It was dark, but he could see flickering lights far away. There was no sound, not even the sound of wind that should have been created by his movement.

During one of his spins (if he *wās* really spinning), he thought he saw the man floating along with him. But the sight lasted only for a second, and he wasn't really sure he'd seen it.

Now some of the lights seemed bigger, and some weren't flickering. They looked like stars.

Could he be floating in space?

He closed his eyes again. Then he heard a sound. It was wind. It was the sound of his own movement.

He opened his eyes and saw that it wasn't dark anymore. Now he could see that he *was* spinning.

He was also falling at an incredible speed, and the ground wasn't very far away. He was about to make contact with an open field near a river.

He caught one more glimpse of the man, falling and spinning like him. Then he closed his eyes tightly, dreading the moment of impact.

It wasn't quite what he had expected. Jeff hit the ground with a tumble, feeling as though he'd only fallen from a ladder about ten feet high. He rolled a few feet, then lay still on his back.

He was surrounded by reeds that must have been almost as tall as he was. He stretched out one arm, then another. Then he did the same with his legs. No pain. Probably no broken bones.

Then he heard a familiar — though not welcome — voice. "Ohhhh!" the man groaned. "Just once, I'd like to land on a haystack. A nice, soft, sweet-smelling haystack."

Jeff sat up, but he couldn't see anything through the reeds. "What happened?" he asked. "Am I — are we *alive* or what?"

He heard a rustling in the reeds, then saw the strange man standing over him.

"Oh, no!" the man said, when he saw who had asked the question. "Yeah, we're alive. And the first thing I have to do is get you back where you belong. Now what year was that?"

He was studying a gold something-or-other strapped to his wrist. All Jeff knew was that it was too big to be a wristwatch.

"Uh — what did you just ask me?" Jeff said.

"What year were we in?" the man said impatiently. "And don't tell me 1492! I know for a fact they didn't have buildings like that in 1492."

"We have them in 1982."

"Look, son —"

"The name's Jeff."

"Jeff. I'm Bogg. And I am not a man who is known for being patient."

"What's that on your wrist?" Jeff asked.

"That's my Omni. And it has circuits that only go as far as 1970. So don't give me any 1982 nonsense, unless —"

He was fiddling with the dials on the Omni, and now he started slapping it with his fingertips.

"It's going berserk again!" he fumed. "I told them to issue me a new one! Bat's breath! Those technicians never listen to anyone but each other!"

"Bat's breath?" Jeff said, grinning.

"Young man, do you have any idea what it's like to repair one of these things in the field? Where's my guidebook?"

He began searching the ground through the tall reeds. Jeff got to his feet. Except for the nearby river, all he could see was miles of more tall reeds.

"Help me look for it," Bogg said. "It has to be around here somewhere."

"Are you talking about a black book?" Jeff asked.

"Yes! Now, look for it! I can't do a thing without it!"

"About this thick?" Jeff said, holding his hands in front of him.

"That's right. You got it?"

"No. Ralph has it."

"Ralph?"

"My dog."

Bogg's face went pale, the way it had been when he looked out at the street.

"Your dog. You mean the big fur coat with all the teeth?"

"Ralph," Jeff said, nodding.

"Ralph," Bogg repeated, the color coming back to his face. "In 1982," he added, the color rising until he was bright red.

He looked at the sky and raised his arms into the air. "Will somebody give me a break?" he pleaded.

Then he turned back to Jeff. As he talked, he slowly moved closer to him.

"Do you know what you've done?" Bogg screamed. "History is going to change because you couldn't control your lousy dog! Empires are going to fall! Wars are going to rage!"

He grabbed Jeff by the collar and then got to the real cause of his anger.

"*I'm* going to lose my job!"

Jeff felt tears welling up, but he wasn't about to let them flow in front of this bully. He tightened his face muscles and stared Bogg in the eye.

"Your job!" he said as loudly as he could. "Who do you think you are? *You* broke into *my* room! *You* knocked *me* out the window! *You* brought me here, wherever I am! You *deserve* to lose your lousy job!"

"Oh, yeah?" Bogg said, threateningly.

"Yeah!" Jeff answered.

Bogg stared silently at him for a few seconds. Then he let go of the collar. He stroked his chin and looked off into the distance.

"Smart kids give me a pain," he said under his breath.

Then they were both startled by a sound neither of them would have expected to hear in this broad, open field. They heard a baby crying.

Bogg began wading through the tall grass. Jeff hesitated for a second, realized he didn't want to be left alone, and followed Bogg.

"Where are we going?" Jeff asked.

"You mean where am *I* going," Bogg said, searching the reeds for the source of the unexpected sound. "*I'm* going to save what's left of my job. *You're* going to get lost."

"I'm lost already."

Bogg ignored him and continued searching. Then he stopped and stared at the water.

Jeff followed his gaze to the edge of the river.

A basket bobbed in the water, caught up in some overhanging reeds. Inside the basket slept a baby, wrapped in a white sheet.

"Is that what we're looking for?" Jeff asked.

They slowly made their way to the basket. Jeff watched as Bogg bent over and looked closely at the baby. The annoyance drained from Bogg's face, and he almost smiled at the infant. Then, remembering that he was being watched, he straightened up and looked businesslike.

He lifted the basket, pulled it free of the reeds, and placed it on dry ground. The baby gurgled happily.

"Well," Jeff said. "Is it?"

"Is it what?"

"What you're looking for."

"I don't know."

"You don't know!"

"I'd know if I had my guidebook. Now I just have to guess."

He began fiddling with the Omni, and Jeff stepped closer to get a look. It did look something like a watch, but instead of a face and hands, it had a small globe.

Around the globe were several rings with numbers in them. In the upper corners were a tiny green light and a tiny red one. The red one was blinking.

Bogg frowned and shook his head. "Nope," he said. "This isn't it."

"It isn't what?"

"It isn't right, that's what!"

"Then what would be?"

"Without my guidebook, I don't know!"

"Look," Jeff said, getting more frustrated by the second, "will you tell me what's going on! I might be able to help you. Who are you? *What* are you?"

Bogg stared down at Jeff for a long time. Then he let out a deep sigh.

"Okay, kid," he said. "I am what is called a Voyager. Ever heard of one?"

Jeff shook his head. Something told him he wasn't going to like this explanation.

"No, of course you haven't," Bogg said. "No one has. We're the folks who are plucked out of our times and trained to travel through the ages. Our job is to help history along. You know, give it a little push when it's needed."

He knelt next to the basket. He reached in and straightened the sheet under the baby's chin. Jeff thought he also saw Bogg throw in a little tickle under the chin, but he couldn't be sure.

Bogg stood up again and half-smiled at Jeff. "The trouble is," he continued, "everything we have to know is in the guidebook."

"But your guidebook —"

"Was your fur coat's dinner. So . . . here I am." He read his Omni. "I'm in Egypt, in 1450 B.C. And I don't have the foggiest idea what I'm supposed to do."

He bent down and picked up the baby. "How about you, kid?" he said, chucking the baby under the chin. "You got an idea?"

"I might," Jeff said softly.

"You? You didn't even know where we were until I told you."

"But I do now. You said we're in Egypt."

"That's right, 1450 B.C."

"We traveled through time," Jeff said.

"Something like that."

Jeff walked over and took the baby from Bogg's arms. "This is Moses," he said.

"Be careful with him," Bogg said. "And stop talking nonsense. Moses is an old man with white whiskers. Looks like Santa Claus with a part down the middle."

Jeff put the baby in the basket. Then he lifted the basket and carried it to the water's edge.

"Hey!" Bogg said. "What are you doing?"

The basket was in the water, already floating downstream.

"He belongs in the water," Jeff said.

"He'll drown!"

"No, he won't. Watch."

Jeff pointed downstream, and Bogg looked. Four people stood on the shore. They wore clothing from ancient Egypt. One of them — a young woman — spotted the basket and called to the others.

Jeff whispered, "Moses was found by the Pharaoh's daughter in the Nile River."

Bogg looked at his Omni. The red light was no longer blinking. The green one glowed steadily.

A grin of amazement crossed Bogg's face. "That did it!" he said happily. "We got the green light. How did you know what we were supposed to do?"

"I know a lot about history," Jeff said, watching the princess carry the baby from the shore. "My father was a history teacher. Can I see that thing?"

He was pointing to the Omni. Bogg's first reaction was to pull his hand behind his back.

"I got you out of this fix, didn't I?" Jeff said.

"Right. You did." Bogg held his arm out so Jeff could get a better look at the Omni. "Just be careful," he added.

Jeff moved closer to look at the rings. He reached out to point at one of them and got closer than he should have.

"Which one do you press to —"

And they were gone. Gone from Egypt, and sailing back into the black void from which they had just escaped.

Chapter 3 _____

Before Jeff even had time to realize what he'd done, they were standing on an open plain.

"You little toad!" Bogg screamed. "Don't you ever, *ever* touch that!"

Jeff barely heard him, because the rumble was so loud. What was that rumble? And why was the ground vibrating?

The answers to both questions came when they looked around. An army of fierce horsemen was closing in on them, less than one hundred yards away. The riders waved swords over their heads and screeched like wounded animals.

Jeff turned in the other direction and saw another army, screaming and charging toward the same point. It was a battle — and they were right in the middle of it.

"Genghis Khan!" Jeff yelled. "Bogg, that's Genghis —"

He couldn't finish because Bogg had hit

the Omni button again. A second before the two armies met head-on, Jeff and Bogg disappeared. A second after that, they fell onto a cobblestone street.

Jeff lay on his back with his eyes closed. His whole body was trembling, as he waited for those crazed warriors to slash him to ribbons. Then he realized that the noise had stopped.

He opened his eyes and moved his body a little. The corners of the cobblestones dug into his back, but he didn't care. The stones told him he was somewhere other than that plain.

Bogg knelt over him and put a hand on his shoulder. "Easy, kid," he said softly. "It's okay. Relax."

"That was —" Jeff stammered. "I mean, we almost —"

"Yes, we almost did," Bogg said, helping Jeff to his feet. "That should give you a pretty good idea why you'll never touch this Omni again."

Bogg cut himself short and gave Jeff a curious look. "What am I saying?" he asked himself out loud. "Look, kid, it's been nice knowing you. Sorry if I've caused you any inconvenience, but I work alone."

He straightened his coat, turned, and walked off down the street. It took Jeff a few seconds to believe what was happening. Then he ran angrily after Bogg.

"Oh, no, you don't, Bogg!" he said, catching up with him. "You got me into this. You're going to get me out. I have to go to school tomorrow!"

Bogg kept walking and didn't even look down at him. "Can't take you back," he said.

"I don't even know where I am!" Jeff cried.

Bogg stopped and checked his Omni. The red light was blinking again.

"France," he said. "1918. Revolutionary War."

"*World War I!*" Jeff said in frustration. "Don't you know anything!?"

Bogg didn't answer because of the explosions. Mortars began blowing up all over the street, and they were surrounded by machine gunfire.

Bogg grabbed Jeff and dived into a stairwell leading to the basement of a house.

As the gunfire continued, Bogg whispered, "What war did you say?"

"World War I," Jeff said. "England, France, and the U.S. against Germany."

"Doesn't sound like a fair fight to me," Bogg said.

"The Germans started it."

"Oh," Bogg said.

An old-fashioned motorcycle careened around a corner into the street where they were hiding. The driver wore a British uniform. Another British soldier was slumped in the sidecar, probably unconscious.

A few seconds behind the motorcycle came a German truck with a machine gunner in the passenger seat. Unfortunately for the

Germans, a horse-drawn lumber cart reached the corner at the same time.

The truck collided with the cart, and the street filled up with loose pieces of lumber. Seeing this, the motorcycle driver stopped right in front of Bogg and Jeff.

"These our side?" Bogg asked.

"Yep," Jeff said.

Bogg ran out to help. The driver turned and fired a revolver in his direction, but missed.

"Put that thing down!" Bogg yelled. "We're on *your* side!"

The driver lowered the gun, probably because Bogg had spoken in English. Now they saw that it wasn't a soldier at all, but a beautiful — really beautiful — young woman in a soldier's uniform.

"Get us out of here!" she pleaded.

Bogg leaped to the sidecar, picked up the wounded soldier, and carried him into the stairwell. Jeff and the young woman followed him down.

He threw his Napoleon coat to the ground, removed the wounded soldier's coat and hat, and put them on. Then he spotted a door leading to the cellar of the building.

"Hide in there," he said.

"Where do you think you're going?" the woman asked.

Bogg put his hands on her shoulders and said, "I'll be back." Then he pulled her close and kissed her.

The woman pulled away and slapped Bogg's face. Bogg looked startled, then confused, then insulted.

"It couldn't have been *that* bad," he said.

Then he ran into the street and hopped on the cycle. The two Germans were free of the lumber now, and they ran toward him. Rifle bullets pinged on the cobblestones around the motorcycle.

Bogg leaned forward and grabbed the handlebars. Then he let out a deep sigh.

"No guidebook," he said.

"The clutch, Bogg!" It was Jeff calling from the stairwell.

Bogg looked over and saw Jeff making a squeezing motion with his left hand. Bogg imitated the motion and the cycle took off down the street.

Jeff and the young woman ducked down as the two German soldiers ran by, firing at the motorcycle.

A few seconds later, they ran by in the opposite direction, this time being chased by the cycle.

Another few seconds and the direction was reversed again, Bogg being chased and fired at by the two soldiers.

One more reversal brought them all back again. This time, the soldiers ran into doorways on either side of the street, and Bogg zoomed right by them. Jeff knew that Bogg couldn't stop the machine. He wondered what the Germans thought was going on.

Now Bogg was headed straight for the mess at the corner. There was lumber all over the street, then the toppled lumber cart, then the German truck.

"Bat's breath!" Bogg screamed.

They watched the cycle approach the lumber. Several pieces formed a ramp, and the cycle shot up into the air. It sailed over the wood, over the cart, and over the truck.

It came down on the other side — right side up — and continued off into the distance. The Germans ran to the truck and took off in pursuit.

Jeff caught his breath. He turned and grinned at the young woman.

"He thinks he's the greatest thing since potato chips, doesn't he?" she said.

"He's not bad," Jeff answered. "Come on, we'd better get inside."

They lifted the wounded soldier and carried him inside the building.

"Do you think he'll come back?" the woman asked.

"He'd better come back," Jeff said.

"Who is he?"

Jeff hesitated only for a moment. Then he said, "He's my father."

Several miles out of town, Bogg tore along a dirt road, the Germans close enough for him to hear their motor. He fiddled with everything he could find on the cycle, but nothing would slow it down.

Suddenly, he saw how his ride was going to end. He was approaching a bridge. So was a mortar, fired by an unseen German gun.

The mortar got there first. It hit the bridge dead center. As the cycle raced toward it, Bogg watched the bridge collapse into the water.

"Doesn't leave me much choice," Bogg muttered, to no one in particular.

There was no way to slow down, so the cycle raced toward the open air that was once occupied by a bridge. The German truck behind him slowed down.

As the cycle soared out over the water, Bogg released his grip on the handlebars and leaned to the side. Thirty feet below, he splashed into the water.

The truck stopped, and the two German soldiers got out. The cycle's forward motion had ended, and they watched it fall into the water.

They waited. Pieces of the demolished bridge floated in the water. The bubbles from the sinking motorcycle disappeared. There was nothing else.

The soldiers smiled and nodded to each other. Then they got into their truck and drove away.

Bogg came bursting to the surface of the water, expecting to be fired at. He faced the sky and gasped for air. No bullets. They'd left him for dead.

"This is my lucky day," he said between gasps.

He began swimming to shore. At every other stroke, his eye was caught by the Omni.

He would have preferred not to think about it. But it was hard to ignore the infernal blinking red light. It meant he had work to do.

Chapter 4 _____

The street at night looked a lot less threatening than it had that day. The cart and all its lumber were gone, and the German truck was off doing damage somewhere else in France.

There were plenty of German soldiers around, but they were more interested in having some fun than in fighting a war.

Several of them were in a tavern at the end of the street, singing songs that reminded them of home. A few had left the tavern to enjoy the cool night air.

At least one soldier seemed to have had too much wine. His uniform was rumpled, and he looked less than military as he tried to weave his way down the street.

Other soldiers made way for him as he wobbled by. He stopped in front of the stairwell that led to the cellar hideaway.

He slumped up against the wall and pushed his helmet back a little. It was Bogg. He looked up and down the street, waiting for a moment when no one was looking at him.

When the moment came, he slipped into the stairwell. It was very dark and very quiet. He slowly opened the door to the cellar. It creaked a lot louder than he would have hoped.

He stepped into the pitch-black cellar and was immediately smacked just below the knees with a heavy board.

A light went on, and he fell to the floor, screaming in pain. He saw the board raised high, ready to come down on his head.

"Bat's breath!" he cried.

"Bat's breath?" Jeff said. "Is that you?"

"No!" Bogg said, getting to his feet. "It's General Eisenhower!"

"Eisenhower?" the woman asked.

"Wrong war," Bogg said.

He rubbed his shins, then straightened up and removed the German overcoat. He looked around and saw piles of old furniture, cardboard boxes, and other discarded belongings. The wounded soldier slept on a cot in the corner of the room.

"Listen," the young woman said, "I'm sorry. First I tried to shoot you, now this. Did we hurt you?"

Bogg smiled, in spite of the sharp pain in his legs. "Hurt me?" he said weakly. "You two?"

He turned and walked toward the cot, gritting his teeth as he tried not to limp. Jeff was standing over the wounded man.

"Where did you get the uniform?" Jeff asked.

"You don't want to know," Bogg said. Nodding toward the soldier, he asked, "How is he?"

"He's better," the woman said. "He's still unconscious, but your son was able to stop the bleeding."

"My *what*?" Bogg asked, glaring at Jeff.

"It was a clean shoulder wound," Jeff said quickly. "His fever is coming down."

"It was terrible," the woman said, sitting on a stool. "We were on our way to entertain the troops, when the zeppelins attacked — bombs everywhere. The corporal took the only road that was open. But it took us behind German lines."

"Do you know who she is?" Jeff asked Bogg.

"No, *son*," Bogg said. "But I'm sure you'll introduce us."

"This is Mary Pickford!" Jeff said. "The most famous movie actress in the world."

"And the most beautiful," Bogg said.

"Mary Pickford!" Jeff repeated. "America's Sweetheart. Miss Pickford, this is — my father."

Bogg turned to her and made a little bow. "Phineas Bogg," he said in his most charming voice.

"*Phineas*?" Jeff giggled behind his hand.

Bogg turned and glared at him. "Phineas," he repeated. Then he turned back to Mary, smiled at her, and kissed her hand.

What he had in mind was holding on to her hand — possibly forever, if the silly look on his face meant anything. She gently removed her hand from his and walked to the other side of the room.

Bogg recovered from the heartbreak. He looked around the room and appeared to be thinking.

"All right," he said to Jeff. "It's obvious that we have to get these folks back where they belong. You watch the corporal. I'll go out and look for a truck."

"I'll go with you," Mary said.

Bogg looked her over. "There are German soldiers out there," he said. "They aren't likely to be kind to someone wearing that uniform you have on."

"Just a minute," she said.

She disappeared behind a high pile of crates. A minute later, she stepped out wearing a skirt and a blouse she'd found in one of the boxes.

"Costumes are my stock in trade," she said. "Let's go."

They walked down the street, Bogg in his German uniform, Mary in the outfit that made her look like every other young woman in the town. They moved slowly and casually, as though they had nowhere in particular to go. As they talked, they kept a sharp lookout for an available truck.

"What is a famous movie actress doing in the middle of the war?" Bogg asked.

"Everyone I know is doing something for

the war effort," she said. "Mostly, they do benefit performances to sell war bonds. I thought I could do more by boosting the morale of the soldiers at the front."

"You certainly boost my morale."

"Thanks," she said, smiling. "Jeffrey told me how you lost your wife."

"Jeffrey?"

"Yes," she said. "I think it's wonderful the way you're bringing him up on your own."

"Oh," Bogg said, feeling pleased with himself. "Well, I really haven't done all that much."

"Modest men are very rare," she said.

"I'm very modest," Bogg said. "Extremely modest, that's what I am."

"If you ever get to Hollywood, I want you to meet my husband."

"Husband?" he said, his face falling.

"He's an actor. You might want to talk to him about a job in the movies. You've saved my life, and I'm sure he'd want to repay you."

"Listen," Bogg said, "could we get back to the modesty part?"

Mary stopped walking and motioned toward something across the street. "Is that what we're looking for?" she asked.

A supply truck sat in front of a small building. Two soldiers leaned on the fenders, apparently waiting for someone.

"Yeah, that's what we're looking for," Bogg said. "Now how do we get it?"

* * *

Back in the cellar, the corporal had come to. Jeff filled him in on what was happening. Then they got around to introducing themselves to each other.

"Eddie Rickenbacker!" Jeff sputtered. "You're Eddie Rickenbacker?"

"That's right," the corporal said weakly.

"You're *the* Eddie Rickenbacker?"

"Sure, I guess so," he said, confused. "Corporal Eddie Rickenbacker. Columbus, Ohio."

"Then what are you doing here?" Jeff asked.

"Lying flat on my back," Eddie said.

"But you're the number one flying ace. You should be up in the air having a dogfight!"

"Dogfight?" Eddie said. "I'm still a little groggy, kid. But I know that dogs don't fight in the air. In the air, they have zeppelins."

"*Zeppelins?*"

"Sure. They look like huge balloons, floating in the air. But they carry bombs, and the Germans are wiping us out with them."

"You mean we're *losing* the war?" Jeff said in disbelief.

"That's right. You can't fight a zeppelin from the ground."

"What about our planes?" Jeff yelled. "You just go up there and shoot the zeppelins down!"

"Planes?" Eddie asked. "You mean aeroplanes? Kid, they can barely get those things off the ground. A guy in France has been working on them for years. All he keeps doing is landing in the English Channel."

31

"A guy in France?" Jeff asked. He was horrified, because he was beginning to understand what was going on. "What about the Wright brothers?"

"Who?"

"Oh, no!" Jeff cried. "That red light must be blinking like crazy!" He ran for the door.

"Hey, kid!" Eddie called. "Where are you going?"

Mary ambled over to the supply truck, while Bogg waited in the shadows. She smiled at the two soldiers leaning on the truck. They smiled back.

She kept walking. Then she pretended to trip and fall. The two soldiers ran to help her. Bogg quietly made his way to the truck. He opened the driver's door and slipped inside. The key was in the ignition.

"Phineas!" Jeff's voice shattered the calm on the street.

"Bat's breath!" Bogg said.

Jeff ran to the truck. The soldiers turned and saw someone sitting it in. Bogg opened the door and pulled Jeff inside.

The soldiers raised their rifles and aimed at the rear of the truck. Mary quietly slipped away at the first sounds of gunfire.

"Still no guidebook!" Bogg said, struggling with the stick shift.

"The clutch!" Jeff yelled, pointing to the floor.

"Again with the clutch," Bogg said.

He jammed his foot on the clutch pedal

and let it out; the truck shifted into gear, and they lurched forward. Other soldiers had come from the buildings, and the truck was being fired on from all angles.

"Your timing could not have been worse!" Bogg said as the truck tore down the street.

"Never mind!" Jeff yelled. "I know what's wrong here!"

"What's wrong is *you*! I have to go back and get Mary!"

He swerved to avoid hitting three people standing in the street. The gunfire was behind them now, but the soldiers would already be in trucks of their own.

"Forget Mary!" Jeff said. "There aren't any airplanes!"

"What are you talking about?" Bogg screamed.

"Airplanes! That's what we have to change! Without airplanes, the Germans are going to win the war!"

They were out of the village now, and Jeff looked ahead to see a German gun truck waiting for them. Bogg spun the wheel and turned off the road.

That left them face to face with a haystack. There was no time to avoid it. The truck went crashing into the hay, then came to a stop.

"What was that they taught us about gear boxes?" Bogg said through clenched teeth. He pushed and pulled the stick, but it wouldn't budge.

"Can you set that Omni to any place and time?" Jeff asked frantically.

"I'm trying to remember my truck mechanics class!" Bogg shouted.

"Never mind the truck! We're losing the war! That corporal with Mary is Eddie Rickenbacker!"

"So?" Bogg asked.

"*So,*" Jeffrey said, hopping up and down in his seat, "he was the top U.S. flying ace in this war. But there aren't any airplanes! He's never even heard of the Wright brothers!"

"That makes two of us," Bogg said. "Now shut up and let me —"

He stopped because of what he saw in the rearview mirror. The gun truck had caught up with them. A dozen soldiers were piling out, rifles raised, and running toward them.

Bogg looked at Jeff and sighed. "The Wright brothers," he said.

"September, 1900!" Jeff said breathlessly. "Kitty Hawk, North Carolina!"

Bogg set the Omni. "Kid," he said, "you better be right. Hang on!"

He pressed the button. They closed their eyes. The German soldiers reached the truck and tore open both doors.

The soldiers stared at the empty seats inside.

Chapter 5 _____

The landing on the beach at Kitty Hawk wasn't bad at all, Jeff thought. Of course, almost anything would have been better than those cobblestones.

The beach was beautiful, and so was the day. There were only three people in sight, surf casters waiting lazily for a bite.

The water was so calm, and the air so still, that Jeff even loosened his hold on Bogg a bit.

Jeff stood on the damp sand, hurling pebbles out over the water. Every once in a while, he'd glance over at Bogg, only half-interested in his progress.

After Bogg had talked to the third fisherman, he walked back to Jeff, kicking wet sand as he moved. He did not look happy.

"Well?" Jeff said.

"Rickenbacker didn't know who the Wright brothers were," Bogg said. "Neither do I. Now, I've found three other people with the same shortcoming."

"They never heard of them?" Jeff said.

"As far as I know," Bogg said, "no one has ever heard of them except *you*."

35

Bogg began walking along the shore, away from the fishermen. Jeff kept up with him.

"Face it, kid," Bogg said, "you made a huge mistake."

"No, I didn't!" Jeff said. "Is your red light blinking?"

Bogg looked at his wrist. "Blinking like crazy," he said.

"Well, try thinking straight!" Jeff said angrily. "It's blinking because something is wrong. What's wrong is that the Wright brothers are supposed to be here, and they aren't. That light won't stop blinking until you get them here."

Bogg seemed to be listening, but Jeff couldn't be sure. After a pause, he added, "So, we have to go to Dayton, Ohio."

Bogg stopped walking and glared down at Jeff. "Dayton?" he yelped.

"That's right," Jeff said, standing his ground.

"First," Bogg said menacingly, "you foul up our escape. Then you make me leave Mary in the middle of World War I. *Then* you drag me halfway across the world to find a couple of guys no one has ever heard of. And *now* you expect me to take you to *Dayton?*"

Jeff didn't back away an inch. "That's where their bicycle shop is," he said.

"No, kid," Bogg said. "This is it. Time for us to part ways. You're in America. It's the same century. And that may be the best I can do." He turned to walk away. "So let's just call it a day."

"Can it!" Jeff screamed, and Bogg stopped walking. "You're stuck with me until you put me back in my room where you found me."

He took advantage of Bogg's hesitation. He stepped in front of him and looked up defiantly.

"Besides," Jeff added confidently, "you don't know anything about history. Without me, you're going to mess everything up."

Bogg looked down at him, with a curious gleam in his eye. The anger was gone. He seemed amused, probably more at himself than anything else. Jeff was relieved that Bogg didn't even try to deny what he'd just said.

Instead, Bogg changed the subject. "What's this 'father' business?" he asked roughly. "I haven't met a woman that beautiful in three hundred years. I don't need you around saying you're my son! What about your own father? What would he say about that?"

"My father is dead," Jeff said.

Carried away by his make-believe anger, Bogg said, "I wouldn't be surprised if you did him in yourself!"

Jeff's eyes widened in horror at what he'd just heard. His face melted into sadness, and his eyes filled up with tears. He turned and ran.

"Hey, kid!" Bogg called. "Wait a minute! I'm sorry! I didn't mean that!"

Jeff kept running, and Bogg took off after

him. He caught up quickly, but he had to tackle Jeff around the ankles to get him to stop.

They fell to the sand, Jeff struggling to get free of Bogg's powerful grip.

"Let me go!" he cried, kicking and punching. "Let me go!"

"Take it easy, young fella," Bogg said tenderly. "Just calm down."

Jeff ran out of strength and stopped struggling. They lay on the sand, the boy sobbing, cradled in the man's arms.

"I'm sorry," Bogg whispered. "I'm really sorry."

When the sobbing subsided, Bogg let him go. He helped Jeff to his feet. Then he knelt in front of him.

"Go ahead and hit me," Bogg said. "I've earned it."

Jeff looked at him for a long moment. Then he lowered his eyes and walked slowly along the shore. Bogg got up and walked alongside him.

"Want to tell me what happened?" he asked.

They walked in silence. Then Jeff let out a deep sigh.

"We were going camping up north," he said. "I was up in the camper reading comic books. My parents were driving. It was my father's turn. I guess he fell asleep at the wheel. We ran off the road and smashed into some trees."

He stopped and looked out over the water.

He was thinking about the accident. Bogg was careful not to make a sound. Then Jeff lay on the damp sand and continued.

"I tried to get them out. But there was this fire. The whole camper was burning. So I ran to the road."

He had his eyes closed now. But the tears made their way out anyway.

"They wouldn't stop. *I couldn't get anybody to stop!*"

Bogg bent down and put a hand on the boy's shoulder. "And you've been blaming yourself?" he said. "You couldn't have done a thing, kid. Not a thing."

He stood and looked out over the water. "You want to talk about blame," he said, "I'll tell you about me and Waterloo. See, Napoleon was never supposed to be there. The guidebook had a plan for the General. This doctor in Paris was supposed to put him in the hospital for his ulcer. Trouble was, I couldn't find the hospital, and —"

He looked down. Jeff was sound asleep, his face streaked with tears.

Bogg took off his coat and carefully laid it over Jeff's small body. He pulled it up over the boy's shoulder, to make sure he wouldn't get a chill.

Then he stood up, shook his head, and smiled. He checked his Omni. The light was still blinking.

"Dayton," he said. "Dayton, Ohio, where we will visit the bicycle shop of the Wright brothers."

Chapter 6 _____

For the first time since he'd met Jeff, Bogg had the leisure to plan where he was going to show up next. So when he punched the date into the Omni, he also punched in an instruction for clothing.

The result was that Jeff and Bogg not only turned up in Dayton, Ohio, in the summer of 1900. They also turned up looking like any other man and boy who might be walking the street in the middle of the day.

Among other things, that meant woolen knickers for Jeff. He didn't like the tight band that held the knickers over his high socks, just below the knee. He *hated* the itchiness of the heavy wool in such warm weather.

Bogg wore a pin-striped suit, a white starched shirt with a high, heavily starched collar, and a wide tie. He looked as though he'd just stepped out of the pages of a 1900 men's fashion magazine.

As they walked slowly along the sidewalk

of a Dayton street, Bogg seemed to be enjoying the role he was playing. Jeff kept stopping to scratch furiously at his legs.

"Will you stop doing that?" Bogg said, annoyed at having his role-playing interrupted.

"I can't help it," Jeff said. "They itch, they're hot, and they make me feel stupid."

"It wasn't my idea to come to Dayton," Bogg said, as they resumed walking.

"No," Jeff said, "but it should have been. What's the Omni doing?"

Bogg looked at it and said, "Red light's blinking away."

"Right," Jeff said. "That means something has to be fixed here." He stopped and smiled at a sign over a store entrance. "And *this* is where it has to be done," he added.

The large overhead sign said, "Wright Cycle Company." In the window near the door, another sign said, "Help Wanted."

"Let's go," Jeff said excitedly, making a beeline for the door.

Bogg took two steps to follow him, then more or less froze in his tracks. A beautiful woman stood in front of the cycle shop. She held a parasol over her head to protect herself from the sun, and she seemed to be waiting for someone.

Bogg stepped up to her and smiled, and she smiled right back. He seemed ready to melt, and it wasn't because of the sun.

"Nice day," he said.

"Yes, it is, isn't it?" she replied.

At the door, Jeff turned and saw what was

happening. "Forget it, Bogg," he called out. "Remember that blinking red light."

Bogg ignored him and made a little bow to the woman. "Phineas Bogg," he said.

She smiled again and said, "Agnes Spence."

There was a pause, during which they stared into each other's eyes. Jeff walked up behind Bogg and pulled on his sleeve.

"Come on, Romeo," he said. "We have work to do."

Bogg looked angrily down at Jeff. Then he looked at the woman again, this time with a slightly embarrassed smile.

"My nephew," he said. He made another little bow and followed Jeff into the store.

It was a cycle store, no doubt about that. But only a few of the cycles looked like Jeff's ten-speed at home. Some of the two-wheelers had one large wheel and one small one. Some of the machines had three wheels, and some had four. Leaning against a wall near the corner were several unicycles.

Jeff reached in and took the "Help Wanted" sign from the window. He handed it to Bogg.

"Tell them you're here for the job," Jeff said.

They could hear the voices of two men from the back of the shop. It sounded very much like an argument.

As they walked to the back, the character of the shop slowly changed. There were fewer cycles back here. Instead, the space was taken up with large blueprints and drawings and with dozens of model planes of various

42

sizes. Against the back wall, just behind the two men, was a full-scale glider.

And there they were in front of the glider — the Wright brothers themselves. As far as Jeff could tell, they might have been two images of the same person, except that one had a mustache.

They were trying to keep their voices down. But it was obvious that they were arguing.

"She *wanted* me to ask her out!" said the one with the mustache.

"She's my girl, Orv!" his brother shot back. In his anger, he threw a coffee cup to the floor.

"It hurts to say this, Will," Orville said. "But she doesn't even *like* you very much."

"That's news to me!" Wilbur said, pushing over a bicycle.

"In fact," Orville said, "she thinks this whole flying idea of yours is crazy and *childish!*"

To emphasize the point, Orville ripped a blueprint from the wall and threw it to the floor.

"Excuse me," Bogg said loudly. "Uh, gentlemen, could I talk to you about the job you have open?"

They both looked at him. "Be right with you," Wilbur said.

Then he turned back to his brother. "*My* idea? Flying is my idea?"

He walked over to a workbench right in front of Jeff. Jeff stared at the dozens of models that covered the workbench. He watched in horror as Wilbur swept them to the floor with his arm.

"*My* idea?" he repeated. "Who spent four sleepless nights designing these wings?"

He picked up a large wing from the floor and bent it in two.

"Who spent ten days flying this box kite?" he fumed, throwing the kite to the floor and stepping on it.

"Who worked for a solid month building this model?" he said, bringing his fist down to smash a six-inch model airplane.

He was momentarily distracted when his fist hit the table, and not the model. Jeff had swiped it away just in time, but Wilbur was too angry to pay him much attention.

"And you're calling *me* childish!" he said, wrapping up his argument.

"Gentlemen," Bogg said loudly. This time they didn't even look at him.

"You think those things are childish?" Orville said, walking to the glider on the back wall. "I'll tell you what childish is!"

As he continued, he tore off pieces of the glider and threw them to the floor.

"*Childish*," Orville said, "is putting a year and a half into a glider that won't fly in a crosswind! Childish is planning to ride this thing off Big Rock Cliff. *Mature* is putting it away before somebody gets hurt!"

As Orville stepped on the last remains of the glider, Bogg looked out the window. Agnes had stopped pacing back and forth. She took a long look inside the store through the window. Then she smiled at Bogg and walked away.

Bogg decided it was time to break things up. He stepped between the two brothers.

"Maybe I *have* matured," Wilbur said.

"Gentlemen," Bogg said, "I think this has gone far —"

He stopped because Wilbur was pulling at a large wing hanging from the ceiling. It would very likely come crashing down on his head, so Bogg stepped out of the way.

"Maybe I'm too mature to care about flying machines," Wilbur said, still tugging at the wing. "Or about younger brothers, or bicycle shops!"

The wing finally came crashing to the floor. Wilbur reached for his hat and his jacket.

Making one last try, Bogg said, "I really don't think Agnes is worth —"

"Maybe I've matured so much," Wilbur said, "that I've had it with the whole kit and caboodle!"

He turned and stomped toward the door. Orville chased after him.

"You don't have the maturity of a billy goat, Wilbur! We're finished, you hear me? You and I are through!"

He kicked over a line of standing bikes near the front door. Then he ran out of the store after Wilbur.

Jeff and Bogg looked at the mess the brothers had left behind. Bogg looked at the "Help Wanted" sign in his hand.

"Why don't I just assume that the job is

mine," he said, tossing the sign onto the pile of debris. "Wish I knew what I had to do, though."

"Sit down, Bogg," Jeff said.

"What?"

"Sit down. I have to fill you in on some elementary facts of American history."

Bogg pulled himself up to his full height. "Who do you think you're talking to, you little tadpole!" he bellowed.

Jeff stared at him. Bogg thought about the blinking red light. Then he thought about what Jeff had just offered. He looked around, spotted a stool, and sat.

Jeff began walking back and forth in front of him, like a college professor giving a classroom lecture. He even stroked his chin to make the imitation a little more realistic. He was obviously enjoying this.

"Now, listen carefully, Bogg, because I'm only going to go over this once. Those two men are the Wright brothers. It was their experiments that led to the development of flying machines. During World War I, American fliers did a lot to help our side win the war. Are you with me so far?"

"I'm with you, kid. Just get on with it."

"In 1918," Jeff went on, "Eddie Rickenbacker *should* be one of the aces who flew American planes against German planes. But the Eddie Rickenbacker we met had never even been in a plane."

"That's because they hadn't been invented,"

Bogg said, pleased that he was finally able to follow all this.

"Right," Jeff said. "But they were *supposed* to be. That's why we came back to 1900. To try to find out why the airplanes weren't on the scene."

"And we've found out," Bogg said. "It's because those two fools started arguing over a woman. And they're about to let that argument get in the way of their work."

"Congratulations," Jeff said. "You've got it. Now, what do you have to do to get that red light to stop blinking?"

"We have to get them back to work on their invention," Bogg said. "We have to get them on their way to Kitty Hawk, North Carolina."

"There's hope for you yet, Bogg," Jeff said tiredly. "Now let's figure out how to get that done."

Chapter 7 _____

Three nights later, they sat in the back of the cycle shop. Bogg was putting the finishing touches on the repair job he'd done on the broken glider. Jeff sat at a desk, writing.

He put the pen down and rubbed his eyes. "Finished," he said. He stood up and walked over to Bogg.

"I just don't know what they see in her," Jeff said. "I mean, she's the cause of all their trouble."

"Oh, don't blame Agnes," Bogg said, stepping back to admire his work. "I had a long talk with her last night. This trouble isn't really her fault."

"Then whose fault is it?" Jeff asked.

"It's nobody's fault, really. This is just a case of three people confused about what they want. Agnes thinks she wants love. But all she really cares about is romance. Orville and Wilbur think they want Agnes. But all they really care about is flying."

He stepped back further, smiled, and took a deep breath. He was pleased with himself.

"Do you think the plan will work?" Jeff asked.

"If I'm right about the three of them," Bogg said, "it'll work. How does it look?" He nodded at the glider.

"It looks terrific. I don't think the brothers could have done better themselves."

Bogg grinned. "Let's hear the notes you wrote."

The next morning, Wilbur Wright woke to find a note on the windowsill of his bedroom. He tore open the note and read it.

"Dearest Wilbur," the note said, "I have so many things to tell you. Orville means nothing to me . . ."

Orville, too, found a note on his windowsill. It was the same, except for a change in names.

"Wilbur means nothing to me," he read. "Meet me at Big Rock Creek at ten o'clock this morning. All my love, Agnes."

At the same moment, Agnes Spence was reading a note that had been left in her mailbox overnight.

"Forget the Wright brothers," she read. "I'll be at Big Rock Creek this morning — waiting to prove my soaring love for you. Yours forever, Phineas Bogg."

The sun was just coming up. Agnes, Orville, and Wilbur each sat at home enjoying a warm glow, as the result of a secret note delivered during the night.

Jeff and Bogg carefully carried the repaired glider from the shop out to a horse-drawn wagon. When they had it firmly in place, they climbed aboard and took off for Big Rock Creek.

An hour later, they stood at the edge of a cliff over Big Rock Creek. The glider was securely tied — for the time being — to the wagon that stood behind them.

The morning sun threw a haze over the horizon, and the air was just beginning to warm up. Jeff and Bogg looked down. It was a drop of about four hundred feet.

Jeff stepped back from the edge, feeling a little dizzy. "It's a long way down," he said lightly.

Bogg swallowed hard, staring into the drop below. "Uh-huh," was the best he could manage.

"Think they'll come?" Jeff asked.

"They'll come," Bogg said, casually stepping away from the edge.

They both looked out at the horizon for several seconds. Then Jeff said, "Think it'll fly?"

Trying to gauge the strength of the breeze fluttering his shirtsleeves, Bogg said, "As long as there isn't a crosswind."

By 9:45, the breeze was stronger. Every once in a while, a strong gust would remind Bogg of the danger of what he was about to do. Bogg didn't need the reminder.

They kept their eyes on the road far below.

Then they saw what they were waiting for. Agnes's carriage was moving slowly up the road toward the creek.

"There she is," Bogg said. "Time to get started."

He went to the wagon and began untying the ropes that secured the glider. Jeff kept watch on the road, ready to keep him posted about the progress of the plan.

Far below the cliff, Agnes sat in her carriage, eagerly anticipating her meeting with Phineas Bogg, the romantic stranger who had happened into her life a few days earlier. The wagon sat in the center of a fork in the road.

She had no idea what was going on four hundred feet overhead, and she couldn't have cared less. She was there to meet Phineas, who had promised to prove his "soaring love" for her.

She heard the gallop of a horse on the road that stretched off behind her, to her right. She decided not to turn around. No sense looking too anxious.

She rested her parasol on her shoulder and waited for Phineas to reach her carriage. Then, the strangest thing happened. She heard another set of hoofbeats, from the road behind her on the left.

Well, one of them was sure to be Phineas. The other would just be somebody riding by.

The first rider reached her carriage, and

the horse pulled up. She turned to face Phineas.

She gave a small gasp when she saw that it was Wilbur. The other rider pulled up, but he wasn't Phineas either.

"Orville!" Wilbur said.

"Wilbur!" Orville said.

"Phineas?" Agnes said, looking in the distance behind each of them.

Four hundred feet above them, Bogg was strapping the last belt of the glider around his waist. The wind was a little stronger now. His toughest job was keeping himself from taking off before he was ready.

"What are they doing now?" Bogg yelled.

"They've both reached her carriage," Jeff said. "The three of them are talking."

Wilbur glared at his brother. Then he looked tenderly at Agnes.

"For you, darling," he said, holding out a box of chocolates, which she took from him. "I'm sorry my brother Orville had to be so immature as to follow me here."

"Follow *you*?" Orville said. "I think it's time we settled this once and for all. Tell him, Agnes."

He held out a bouquet of flowers, which Agnes took from him.

"Tell him what?" she asked, glancing at each of the roads behind them.

"Tell him about the note you wrote me," Orville said.

"What note, Orville?" she asked.

"The one telling me to meet you here."

"She wrote *me* that note!" Wilbur said.

Jeff could see that the three people were all yelling about something. He knew what that meant.

"The cat's out of the bag," he said.

"Okay," Bogg said. "Time to go."

"Are you kidding?" Jeff said. "There's too much wind!"

"I didn't set up this meeting for my health, kid."

He moved toward the edge, the glider strapped to his back. Because of the wind, his progress was very, very slow.

"You can't, Bogg! Not in a crosswind!"

"I have to, kid. They aren't going to stay down there forever. Now, step out of the way."

"It's suicide!" Jeff yelled.

"I'm a Voyager, kid. Sometimes you have to bite the bullet and do what has to be done."

He moved farther toward the edge, and the wind got stronger.

"No!" Jeff yelled. He leaped for Bogg's ankles.

Bogg sidestepped him and stood at the edge. He looked down, took a deep breath, then leaped out into space.

Jeff stood watching in horror, as the glider sank straight down.

Chapter 8 _____

Down, down, down the glider went, picking up speed as it dropped. The first hundred feet didn't scare Bogg much. The second hundred made him think he'd lost his mind. Now, more than halfway to the ground, he was sure of it. This wasn't flying! It *was* suicide!

Then the wind decided to stop toying with him. He felt a bone-wrenching jerk, and suddenly, he wasn't falling anymore. The glider straightened out, and Bogg was flying.

Like a huge bird, he sailed out over the open field. His fear drained away, then was replaced by giddiness.

He let out a whoop as the wind lifted him into an arcing curve. He shifted his weight and found that he could actually control the direction of the curve. That called for another whoop.

While Phineas Bogg was having the time of his life, Jeff was already in the wagon, whipping the horse into breakneck speed. All

Jeff had seen was Bogg plummeting toward the ground. He drove the wagon down the long road toward the bottom of the cliff.

"This is *not* my handwriting!" Agnes said insistently, staring at the two notes Wilbur and Orville had handed her.

Orville sputtered, "Then who in tarnation —"

"Look!" Agnes pointed at the sky.

The brothers looked up. They saw the glider, dipping and turning, hundreds of feet up in the air.

"That's who wrote the notes!" Agnes said.

"Who?" Wilbur yelled.

"Phineas!" Agnes said, holding her hands near her heart. Then, quoting from his note to her, she added softly, . . . "waiting to prove my *soaring* love for you!"

"The glider!" Orville gasped. "Will, that's *our* glider!"

"And it's *flying*!" Will shrieked.

Wilbur and Orville turned their horses and took off across the field. Agnes followed slowly in her carriage. Jeff, in the wagon, reached the bottom of the hill and followed Agnes.

High in the sky, Bogg decided he'd proved his point. It was time to get this thing on the ground. But that proved to be a lot harder than he'd expected it to be.

Even after so short a flight, Bogg had a good sense of how to make the glider go left or right. The gusts of wind had sent it up three or four times already. *Down* was something else again.

He tried moving his body into every angle he could manage. He did manage to dip once, but it turned out to be only the beginning of a long, slow rise.

"Doesn't this thing ever go down?" Bogg screamed.

As though in answer, the wind suddenly died.

"I had to ask," he muttered.

The glider was on its way down. Bogg wasn't plummeting headfirst, as he had at the beginning of the flight. But he was moving even faster, and he was headed straight for a clump of trees.

On the ground, his audience was assembled. There was nothing any of them could do but wait and see how it would turn out.

Orville cupped his hands and hollered, "Get your weight back!"

"Phineas!" Agnes yelled. "Be careful!"

"Hang on, Bogg!" Jeff called.

But they all knew that Bogg couldn't hear a word they were saying. And all they could do was watch and wait.

The glider was moving even faster now. Bogg realized he'd completely lost control. When the trees were less than fifty yards away, he prepared himself for the worst.

"Bat's breath!" he said, as though it somehow summed up his whole life.

The glider crashed into the trees, pieces of wing flying off in all directions. There were loud sounds of ripping and crunching. Rushing to the scene, Jeff prayed that was only canvas and wood he heard, not skin and bone.

They all ran to the trees. Jeff got there first. He saw canvas and broken struts in the trees and all over the ground. Then he spotted the pilot, sprawled over a large piece of wing.

"Bogg!" Jeff ran to him, as Agnes and the brothers approached the clearing. "No, Bogg! You can't die!" Jeff cried, fighting his way through the wreckage.

Bogg still had the straps around his arms and waist, but they'd been torn loose from the glider itself. Jeff pushed his way to Bogg, tears running down his face.

He grabbed the man's feet and tried to pull him free of the wreckage.

"You can't die!" he kept repeating. "You can't die!"

He tugged at the feet. Bogg's head fell to the ground.

"Ouch!"

Jeff stopped tugging. "Bogg?" he said tentatively.

Bogg moaned. Jeff let go of his feet, sending them thumping to the ground.

"Easy, kid," Bogg mumbled. "You always treat your friends like this?"

Jeff threw himself over Bogg's body and hugged him. Bogg intended to return the hug. The best he could do was to lift one arm and let it fall over Jeff's back.

"Bogg!" Jeff sobbed. "I saw you crash! I thought . . ."

"I know, kid, I know," Bogg whispered. "I'm glad to see you, too."

"Phineas!" Agnes said lovingly.

Bogg opened his eyes. There was Agnes, standing over him.

Jeff got up and helped Bogg get slowly to his feet. The Wright brothers stood by, trying to make some sense out of what was going on.

When Bogg was standing, Agnes threw her arms around his neck and splattered his face with kisses.

"Phineas," she said between kisses. "It was wonderful . . . your soaring love . . . are you all right?"

Bogg freed himself from her grip. "A little worse for wear, darling," he said. "But now I know more than ever that I want to marry you."

She stepped back, eyes wide with astonishment. "Marry me!" she said.

"We'll grow old together," Bogg said. "You and me and the ten children."

"The . . . ten . . . children?" Agnes said uncertainly.

"We'll be deliriously happy," Bogg went on. "Traveling all over the country . . ."

"Traveling?" she said weakly.

"Of course," Bogg said. "I'm going to take this glider show to every town in the U.S. of A.!"

He turned and winked at Jeff, as Agnes backed off in the direction of her carriage. Wilbur and Orville, who had watched the whole scene, stepped up to him.

"First you steal our glider," Wilbur said angrily, "and *wreck* it! Then you steal our girl!"

"We ought to shoot you right here!" Orville threatened.

Bogg looked from Wilbur to Orville, then back to Wilbur again. His eyes crinkled. His mouth began to turn up. Then his face broke into a grin. Orville and Wilbur grinned, too.

"Dang!" Wilbur said, extending his hand. "That was beautiful!"

"Thanks," Bogg said, shaking hands with him.

"We owe you a lot," Orville said, offering his hand. Bogg shook it.

"You know," Wilbur said, "the problem you had up there was lift."

Orville picked up a piece of the broken wing. "We have to make the elevators a little bigger," he said.

"And mount them further forward," Wilbur added. "Don't you think so?"

They were examining pieces of the wreckage now. Bogg and Jeff — and Agnes apparently — were completely forgotten.

"I was thinking," Orville said, "if we stacked the wings . . . maybe extended them a bit —"

"But we can't test it here," Wilbur said. "We'll need a longer run and steady winds."

"There's that place Chanute recommended," Orville said. "In North Carolina. Kitty Hawk, wasn't it?"

They drifted away, carrying pieces of the wreckage with them. Jeff and Bogg looked at each other. They both smiled. Then Bogg checked the Omni.

"Green light, kid," he said happily.

Jeff's smille faded. He looked upset. "We can't leave now," he said.

"Have to, kid. We're due back in France, 1918. Remember?"

"But they're about to invent the airplane, Bogg! We can be there! We can help!"

"The light's green, kid. We've given them all the help they need."

Jeff looked after the brothers, riding away on their horses. He sat on the ground, very close to tears.

"Look, I know it's hard," Bogg said tenderly, sitting next to him. "Nobody knows it better than I do. But when you feel this way, you have to think of all the interesting people and places in *front* of you, who really need your help."

He stood up. He offered his hand to help Jeff stand along with him.

"We're Voyagers, kid. We have responsibilities."

Jeff gave him a sad smile and nodded.

"Besides," Bogg said brightly, "don't you want to see what all this has done for history?"

The sadness slowly gave way to curiosity. "Yeah," Jeff said. "Yeah, I do."

"Phineas?" They turned to see Agnes sitting in the carriage. She was facing off to the side, unwilling to look him in the eye with the bad news.

"Phineas," she repeated, "I've thought this thing over. I'm not sure I'm ready for marriage."

She turned to face her daring suitor. There was no one there. She ran her eyes over the whole scene of the wreckage.

The man and the boy had disappeared. "Can you imagine that?" Agnes said out loud.

Chapter 9 _____

A tired old horse stood in front of a pile of hay, making the best of the only food available. The hay stood outside the remains of a barn. It had recently been all but destroyed by German mortars.

The barn belonged to a farm, not far from the French village Bogg and Jeff had left behind. The farm was one of the victims of World War I.

A whistling sound pierced the air and very quickly became louder and louder. The horse had heard enough mortars recently to recognize the sound as dangerous. It trotted off in the direction of a nearby field.

The whistle became louder — louder — ear-shattering. But no explosion came. Instead, Jeff and Bogg flew through the air onto the pile of hay. The whistling came to an end.

Bogg stretched out his arms and legs and smiled in the direction of the sky. "A soft landing at last!" he exclaimed.

Jeff sat up and looked around. He brushed some hay from his hair and shoulders.

"Green light?" he asked.

Bogg looked at the Omni. "Nope," he said. "Blinking red."

Sitting on top of the mound of hay, they couldn't see the plane in the distance behind them. It was headed straight at them.

"How could it be red?" Jeff said. "We put Orville and Wilbur on the right track! It *had* to work!"

"The red light could mean something else is wrong," Bogg said calmly. "We'll find out soon enough."

It turned out to be sooner than he thought. The red plane was nearly upon them, and it opened fire.

Clumps of hay spat into the air as the machine gun bullets tore into the mound.

Bogg moved with his usual swiftness, even though he had no idea what was happening. He grabbed Jeff's arm and pulled him from the mound down to the ground.

The plane was ahead of them now, rising from its dive. They scrambled into the half-demolished barn and looked up at their attacker.

"Terrific!" Bogg bellowed. "Wonderful! We get airplanes into the war so they can blow us to bits!"

"It's red!" Jeff said excitedly.

"What is?" Bogg asked, staring after the plane.

"The *plane* is red," Jeff answered.

"Of course it is! I can see that! What about it?"

"It must be von Richtofen," Jeff said, looking up in awe.

"Richtofen?" Bogg said. "The guy with Mary?"

"That's *Rickenbacker*," Jeff said slowly, as though he were talking to a child. "Von Richtofen is a *German* ace. He's the Red Baron!"

The plane was out of sight now. Jeff was about to explain who the Red Baron was, when he looked out the other side of the barn.

"Look!" he cried.

Two biplanes sat side by side in a field. They could see four people, and two of them seemed to be wounded. The other two were dragging them in the direction of a wooded area.

Bogg and Jeff ran in their direction. When they got closer, they saw that the two healthy ones weren't strangers.

"Eddie!" Jeff panted.

"Mary!" Bogg said.

They ran faster. As they got closer, Jeff recognized the two planes. He'd seen pictures in his World War I history books.

They were both two-seaters. Both had the markings of the 94th Aero Squadron. One of the planes had a machine gun mounted in the rear.

"Eddie!" Jeff called. "Mary!"

The four people stopped and turned. Eddie and Mary lowered the two men to the ground.

The upper part of Eddie's right sleeve was covered with blood. Jeff and Bogg ran up to them, Jeff calling their names over and over. Eddie and Mary stared at them in confusion.

"Who are you?" Eddie asked.

"Who am I? I'm Jeff. Jeff Jones!"

"No good, kid," Bogg said softly. "That was another world — that's why they don't remember us."

He stepped forward and held out his hand to Rickenbacker. "I'm Phineas Bogg," he said. "This is my son, Jeff."

Jeff's eyes lit up. He stood a little more erect, proud to hear himself referred to that way. Bogg and Rickenbacker shook hands.

"We're here to help you get out," Bogg said. Then he asked, "Are you okay?" motioning toward Eddie's bleeding arm.

Eddie looked in the direction of the two soldiers under the tree. "I'm alive," he said simply.

They were interrupted by the roar of an engine overhead. They looked up to see von Richtofen's plane bearing down on them.

"Hit the deck!" Eddie roared.

The four of them fell face down on the ground. The plane swooped down on them, passing over the four figures not fifteen feet off the ground.

The noise was deafening, and the wind created by the plane didn't help matters. But

Jeff and Bogg were waiting for a burst of machine gunfire, and it never came.

They looked up to watch the plane soar back into the sky. As they did, they saw something fall from the cockpit.

"Why didn't he fire?" Mary asked, getting to her feet.

"He wants me," Rickenbacker said. He got up and stared after the plane. Then he walked over and picked up the thing that had dropped from the plane.

It was a black leather glove. Eddie held it high for the others to see.

"It's a challenge," he said. "From the top German ace to the top American ace."

Jeff stepped forward, a worried look on his face. "You can't fight him in one of these," he said, gesturing toward the two planes. "He'll destroy you!"

"Don't worry, kid," Bogg said. "He isn't going to." To Eddie, he said, "Take off your jacket and scarf. At this distance, he'll never know the difference."

Eddie stared at him for a few seconds, then smiled a little. "Forget it, pal," he said.

Bogg stepped up to him and grabbed the wounded arm. Eddie winced in pain.

"You're in no shape to take him on," Bogg said. "Maybe if you had your own plane, but not in one of these crates."

Eddie looked thoughtfully at the two planes. Then he looked at his bleeding arm.

"You fly Mary out of here," Bogg said. "We'll take care of the Baron."

Eddie hesitated, trying to weigh all the factors. Bogg didn't want to give him a chance to think too long about the decision.

"You can get Mary out of here alive," Bogg said. "That makes it worth a shot."

Eddie nodded, then pulled off his scarf and his jacket. Bogg put them on quickly. Then he took the leather glove that Eddie held out to him.

"You know how to fly one of these?" Eddie asked.

Bogg chuckled. "Did Benjamin Franklin know how to write?" he asked.

He looked up in the sky. There was no sign of the Red Baron just now.

"Suppose we let you go up first," Bogg said. "Will he wait for me?"

"Yes," Eddie said. "The Baron doesn't fire on unarmed planes. It's part of his code of honor. He'll let us pass."

"Then get a move on," Bogg said.

Eddie started toward the plane. Then he turned back to Bogg and held out his hand. Bogg grasped it.

"Good luck, pal," Eddie said.

Mary bent down to face Jeff. She kissed him on the nose.

"I don't know who you are, kid," she said. "But thanks a million. And good luck."

She stood and walked to Bogg, who was standing near the armed plane. They gazed into each other's eyes.

"I have the funniest feeling that we've met," she said.

Bogg laughed softly. "Maybe in another life," he said.

She stepped up to him and they kissed. Then he helped her into the plane, where Eddie was waiting to take off.

They watched the plane taxi out onto the field. Then it began a straight run, going faster and faster, until it was off the ground. Mary and Jeff waved to each other.

When the plane was almost out of sight, Jeff said, "Why did you lie to him? You couldn't even fly the glider!"

"I didn't lie," Bogg said, buttoning up his pilot's jacket. "I never lie. Did you ever try to read Benjamin Franklin's handwriting?"

Chapter 10 _____

Bogg made a move to get into the pilot's seat, when he saw Jeff headed for the rear seat. He grabbed Jeff's arm to stop him.

"Climb down, kid!" he said angrily. "I'm doing this flight solo!"

"No!" Jeff said defiantly. "If you go down, I go down!"

"Forget it!" Bogg said, turning back to the plane.

"Who's going to fire the gun?" Jeff yelled. "It's in the rear!"

"No discussion!" Bogg said, since he had no answer for that elementary question. "That's it!"

Jeff watched as he climbed into the cockpit, put on Eddie's helmet, and adjusted the goggles. Then he reached uncertainly for the controls.

"Now," he said, trying to sound much more confident than he was. "Where's the clutch?"

Jeff let a few seconds go by. Then he said,

"It doesn't have a clutch." He climbed into the gunner's seat.

"Smart kids give me a pain," Bogg mumbled.

"Pull out the throttle," Jeff instructed.

As they taxied, Bogg looked up into the sky. The Red Baron's plane was waiting for them. It circled overhead. Bogg thought of vultures.

The plane raced down the field, picking up speed. Bogg sang out, "Remember the *Maine*!"

"Wrong war again!" Jeff yelled over the sound of the engine. Then he saw the trees up ahead.

The speed of the plane was increasing, and the space available for takeoff was decreasing. If they weren't off the ground in a few seconds, they'd run smack into one of those trees.

"The stick!" Jeff called.

"What stick?" Bogg screamed in panic.

Jeff stood up, leaned over toward the cockpit, and pointed. "Pull back on the stick!"

Bogg did as he was told, and the plane began to rise. "OH!" Bogg cried in relief. "*That* stick!"

They grazed the tops of the trees and continued rising. Bogg held the stick back with all his weight.

"I'm flying!" he sang.

The angle of the plane got sharper and sharper, until it was moving straight up. Then it began to loop. It slowly turned over, so that Bogg and Jeff had to look *up* to see the ground.

Fortunately, the Red Baron couldn't hear the groans and screams coming from the American plane. He must have thought Rickenbacker was giving him a little show of his flying ability.

It was also fortunate that the plane came out of the loop on its own. When it straightened out, Bogg took control of the stick, and they flew level.

Just as he started feeling pleased with himself, they were given a reminder of why they were up there in the first place. A round of machine gunfire tore a series of holes into the canvas on the side of the plane.

Von Richtofen blasted past them and prepared for another attack. He was behind them now, and Jeff knelt on his seat to man the machine gun.

"Here he comes!" Jeff screeched. "Pull up! Get above him! Keep him off our tail!"

Bogg's eyes were wide with terror as he pulled gently back on the stick. The plane began to rise, but von Richtofen stayed right with them.

"Pull up!" Jeff yelled.

"I can't pull up anymore!"

"Then push it down!"

Bogg followed the instruction, and the plane dipped. The Baron was close behind now, and Jeff fired the machine gun.

"Shoot him!" Bogg yelled.

"I am shooting him!"

"Then *hit* him!"

And that's exactly what Jeff did. A round of bullets shredded a section of the Red Baron's right wing.

The Baron's plane teetered from side to side. The wing began smoking, then burst into flame.

"I got him!" Jeff cried. "I got him!"

The Baron tipped his wings in salute to the American ace. Then he turned and began a slow descent to safety.

Bogg watched giddily as the German ace retreated. "You did!" he yelled. "You got him!"

He checked his Omni and grinned. Then he held it up for Jeff to see.

"Green light, kid!" he called over his shoulder. "History is back on course! We did it! We —"

His joy faded as he looked at his own left wing. It was on fire.

The plane dipped, then went into a tailspin. They were falling toward the ground at an incredible speed.

Bogg tried every control he could get his hands on. Nothing worked, and the plane continued to fall.

He reached his arms back. "Hold on to me, kid!" he screamed. "Hold on!"

Jeff fought his way out of the seat and grabbed onto Bogg's shoulders. Bogg struggled to set the Omni.

They were only a few feet from the ground

when Bogg finally pressed the Omni button. There was a terrific jolt. But no crash.

They fell from the sky and landed softly on a grassy plain. They opened their eyes and looked around.

No flames. No crushed plane. No blood, and no broken bones. Just a lovely green countryside.

Chapter 11 _____

"**W**e *are* alive, aren't we?" Jeff asked.

"Yeah," Bogg said. "We made it."

"And Eddie and Mary?"

"Green light, kid, remember? They made it, too."

"Good," Jeff said.

Bogg stood over Jeff, staring down at him thoughtfully.

"Time to talk business, kid," he said.

"What kind of business?"

"I have to get you home."

"Home? But we're Voyagers."

"*I'm* a Voyager, kid. You're only here by accident."

"But . . . you can't" Jeff said. "You told me your Omni can only be set as late as 1970."

"Not true," Bogg said. "I have an adapter to bring it up the the twenty-fifth century. I didn't have much faith in the adapter, because the Omni was fouled up. But it's been working perfectly the last few times."

"But, Bogg," Jeff pleaded. "I don't want to go home."

"I know, kid," Bogg said tenderly. "And you must know by now that I don't want you to go. But rules are rules."

"*What* rules?"

"You have to be called to be a Voyager, kid. You have to be plucked out of time and assigned the job."

"How do I get called?" Jeff asked.

"I don't know," Bogg said. "But I do know one thing. When I turn in my report, your name will go to the top of the list of candidates. They won't even have to train you."

"You think they'll call me?" Jeff asked.

Bogg smiled at him. "They'd be crazy not to," he said.

They stood there smiling at each other. Then they heard a booming sound from far off.

"Hear that?" Bogg said. "It sounded like a cannon."

There was another explosion, this time much closer. Then they heard the sound of hundreds of hoofbeats.

"Where are we?" Jeff asked, looking around.

Bogg checked the Omni. "England," he said. "1066. Pearl Harbor."

More explosions. "They didn't have cannons in 1066!" Jeff said.

"They had plenty at Pearl Harbor," Bogg said uncertainly.

Another explosion. "The Battle of Hastings!" Jeff said.

"What?"

"England, 1066!" Jeff said excitedly. "The Battle of Hastings! There aren't supposed to be cannons here!"

A cannon shell exploded twenty feet behind them. They fell to the ground and covered their heads.

"No cannons, you say?" Bogg asked.

"That's right! We have to get rid of those cannons!"

They stood up and looked at the top of a nearby hill. There, heading for them at a fierce pace, rode William the Conqueror and his Norman army.

As they scrambled for cover, Bogg yelled, "Looks like your return trip is going to be delayed a little, kid!"

Jeff ran for the trees, grinning and giggling all the way.